THE POLAR EXPRESS
THE MOVIE

KEEPSAKE MEMORY BOOK

WRITTEN
BY
MELISSA MORGAN AND HEIDI CHO

BASED ON THE MOTION PICTURE SCREENPLAY
BY
ROBERT ZEMECKIS AND WILLIAM BROYLES, JR.

BASED ON THE BOOK *THE POLAR EXPRESS*,
WRITTEN AND ILLUSTRATED
BY
CHRIS VAN ALLSBURG

DESIGN
BY
DOYLE PARTNERS

HOUGHTON MIFFLIN COMPANY, BOSTON

L ate one Christmas Eve, many years ago, a young boy was awakened by the sound of a train hissing to a halt outside his bedroom window. The train was the Polar Express, which waited to take the boy on a journey to the North Pole. The boy had been specially chosen for the trip so that he could search for answers to his questions about Santa Claus and the true meaning of Christmas. During this trip the boy met people and saw places that filled his eyes and mind with wonder and excitement, and taught him valuable lessons of friendship and faith. Most important, the journey to the North Pole gave the boy a chance to believe in the magic of Christmas once again.

This is a keepsake book of the boy's memories of his adventure that one enchanted night, many years ago.

All aboard the
Polar Express!

BALDWIN LOCOMOTIVE WORKS

One of the most famous and successful steam locomotive manufacturers in the world was called BALDWIN LOCOMOTIVE WORKS of Philadelphia. Baldwin was the largest locomotive builder in the nineteenth century. Baldwin was well known for its incredibly fast production rates—a single engine took the factory only eight short weeks to build, from beginning to end. How was it possible for Baldwin to produce their magnificent steamers at such unbelievable speed?

The secret was in the many thousands of workers employed to make the most magnificent steam engines around. It was the extraordinary work of specialists like blacksmiths, drillers, pipe fitters, draftsmen, painters, and machinists that all came together in the final stages of fitting together each locomotive. In fact, the frames and machined parts built by these craftsmen were made so precisely that, inside an erecting shop an entire city block large, it took an army of 3,200 workers only about one short week to fit together all the parts! At that rate it's no surprise that the company, established in 1831, built about 75,000 locomotives from the day it opened until it closed its doors in 1956.

POLAR EXPRES

You might take **trains** for granted, but they're only about 200 years old!

THE STEAM LOCOMOTIVE

In 1804 the invention of the locomotive changed the way people lived. This new "speedy" train travel made it possible for people to live much farther from their workplaces, and to visit faraway places in a much shorter period of time. And because the trains carried goods as well as people, it became possible to buy things like fresh fruits and vegetables far from where they were grown!

One of the first locomotives ever built for commercial transportation was named the Rocket, and it traveled at twenty-nine miles per hour. That may not sound very fast to us now, but remember that before these early trains were invented, the fastest way for groups to travel was on a trolley car pulled by mules or horses! In fact, this high-speed train travel was once considered so technologically advanced that one scientist thought that the speed could make people's brains fall out!

THE ROCKET.

e speed
ed. This
ade it
uch
s, and to
n shorter
the
danger,
gs
far
One
for
gravity
epths
ound
er
re
ups
led
high
ght
l
e
lift

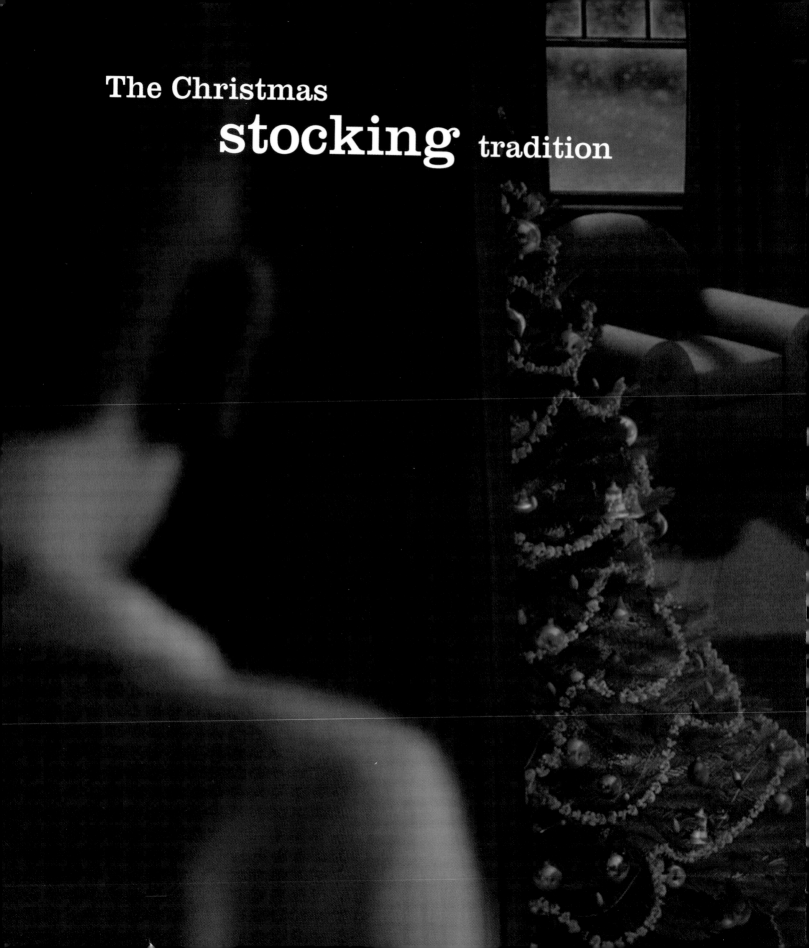

The Christmas stocking tradition

THE LEGEND OF THE CHRISTMAS STOCKING

Once upon a time and long ago there was a very kind but poor nobleman who had three grown daughters. When it came time for his daughters to marry, the nobleman became very unhappy because he didn't have enough money to provide dowries for their weddings. One night, after the daughters had washed out their clothing, they hung their stockings over the fireplace to dry as they always did, and went off to bed. That same night, Christmas Eve, while the family was asleep, Saint Nicholas peered into the window and saw the daughters' stockings hanging by the fire. Knowing the despair of their father, Saint Nicholas took three small bags of gold from his pouch and threw them carefully, one by one, down the chimney and into the drying stockings. The next morning when the daughters awoke, they each found enough gold for them to get married. The whole family was overjoyed, and a new Christmas tradition was born!

Children all over the world continue the tradition of hanging Christmas stockings or practice similar customs. In France and Scandinavia, kids place their shoes by the fireplace in hopes of finding them filled with goodies on Christmas Day. Children in Hungary even polish their shoes so they will be shiny before setting them out near the door or on a window-sill, hoping to find them filled with treats in the morning!

It's snowing! It's snowing!

DO YOU KNOW THAT IF YOU STICK OUT YOUR TONGUE TO CATCH A SNOWFLAKE, YOU'RE PROBABLY EATING DUST?

That's right! Almost every snowflake that falls starts off as a tiny speck of dust swirling around high in the sky. When the dust speck flies deep inside a cloud, water vapor clings to it and freezes, holding fast. This icy fleck then starts to bump into other frozen crystals, and they freeze together, forming bigger crystals. Each snowflake is made up from two to about two hundred separate ice crystals. When the flake becomes heavy enough, it ends its long journey by floating softly to the ground. There, it can become part of a fort, a snowball, or even a snowman!

PROJECT

Do you believe that no two
snowflakes are alike?
See for yourself!

1. All you need to catch some falling
snowflakes is a strip of dark fabric that's
been out in the cold for ten minutes (so
the snowflakes don't melt when they land).

2. During the next snowfall, go outside
and hold the fabric taut. Catch as many
flakes as you can, then use a magnifying
glass to examine the snowflakes up close.
Notice the variety of unique, beautiful
patterns you've captured.

3. If you want, you can sketch the shapes
into a notebook and compare the patterns
to see how they're similar and how they're
different!

Snowflakes might be good at sticking together,
but each is definitely one of a kind. No two
snowflakes look exactly alike—each one has
six sides but is beautiful and unique with its
own special design. The shape that a flake will
be depends on the temperature that it forms in!
The colder it is outside, the smaller and more
intricately patterned the snowflake will be.

There's nothing better on a trip to the North Pole than a nice cup of **hot chocolate!**

THE POLAR EXPRESS
HOT CHOCOLATE

PER PORTION

1 generous cup of wholesome milk
1 very generous teaspoon of chocolate
(powdered or syrup)

ON THE STOVETOP

Add ingredients to a saucepan
and heat on low, stirring until steam rises.
(Do not overheat.)

Pour into a mug.

IN A MICROWAVE

Pour ingredients into a mug.

Heat and stir.

For a holiday treat, add a candy cane or
cinnamon stick when serving. Enjoy!

WHEN HOT CHOCOLATE WAS REALLY HOT

The Aztecs, an ancient Mexican civilization, used to make their "hot" chocolate cold and flavored with wine and hot chili peppers! Imagine what that tasted like! That was the first form of chocolate ever discovered by Europeans, and that's the way it was introduced to Spain in the early 1500s by the explorer Hernan Cortes.

The Spaniards quickly adopted the exciting new drink but changed it a little and made it like we do, serving it hot and sweetened—without the chili peppers. They kept this wonderful discovery a huge secret, protecting it for centuries before the recipe leaked to neighboring countries like England in the 1700s. Hot chocolate became a big hit in London, where "chocolate houses" were established to serve the drink. It was the English who started to add milk to the chocolate mixture, making it lighter and more similar to the hot chocolate we enjoy today!

What are those glowing eyes out in the snow?
Wolves!

Wolf *(cont'd)*

6. Wolf Packs.— A group of wolves that lives and plays together, like a family, is called a pack. Packs can be as small as just two members, or as big as thirty—but they usually have about six to eight members. Pack life makes it easier for wolves to raise their young and, more important, hunt for food.

7. Arctic Wolves.— The wolves that live near the North Pole are called Arctic wolves, and they're a little different from the gray wolves that live in warmer environments. These wolves are slightly smaller than their gray relatives, weighing up to 110 pounds and measuring about 5 feet from the tip of their nose to the tip of their tail. To help reduce heat loss in their chilly surroundings, they have more rounded ears, a shorter muzzle, and shorter legs. They also have hair between the pads of their feet to help them walk through snow.

Arctic wolves' most special feature is the long, thick, snowy white fur that makes them seem to disappear right into their surroundings. These wolves look as if they've been dipped into a pile of pure snow! This perfect camouflage—along with big sharp teeth and a great sense of sight, smell, and hearing—makes white wolves excellent hunters. These animals are brave! They run at speeds of up to 35 miles per hour to hunt animals that are many times their size, like the giant musk ox! But there's no need for us to be scared—wolves almost never attack people!

Wom'bat, n. *(Zoöl.)*
The common name of the *Phascolomydae*, a family of *Rodentia*, comprisint quadrupeds which have large, flat heads, short legs and a body that appears as if crushed

Can you tell if that animal with the big velvet-covered antlers is a **reindeer**, or a **caribou**?

That's a trick question, because the answer is it's both! In some parts of the world, like Alaska and Canada, people refer to wild reindeer as caribou—but both names describe the same animal.

Reindeer are members of the deer family that have adapted special physical features to live in cold, snowy climates like the Arctic. Each hair in their outer coat is hollow and traps warm air, keeping the reindeer warm—but still allows them to lie down in the snow without melting it! Thick fur even covers their muzzles, which they use to burrow under the deep snow to find their favorite food—lichens called "reindeer mosses."

Reindeer are herbivores, which means they munch on only plants, like willow leaves, lichens, mushrooms, and small shrubs such as blueberry. But because these animals are plant eaters, they're always on the move in search of enough food to eat. Reindeer migrate in herds that travel south for the winter and north for the summer. Experts think they have a built-in compass, just like migratory birds, because they can travel through unfamiliar areas to reach the same grounds year after year.

THE POLAR EXPRESS

There's a reason Santa chose reindeer to be his special helpers. Aside from being well equipped to make long journeys, these animals are strong working and can pull a sled twice their own weight. With some reindeer weighing as much as 700 pounds, just imagine how many toys one reindeer can draw at once!

Did you know that there are different types of ice?

✳DESTINATION

THE POLAR EXPRESS
NORTH POLE ✳

You might think of ice only as the stuff that cools your lemonade, but near the North Pole, ice is often all you see for miles ahead! Ice makes up most of the Arctic's landscape, and people who have visited are usually amazed by the many kinds of ice in the region.

A few types of ice have some pretty strange names; one of these is pancake ice. Pancake ice is thin, very flat, and is the first layer of ice that freezes atop a body of water. Its name comes from the fact that it lies in pieces across the water's surface, just like separate pancakes sizzling away in a skillet! Growler ice is the name given to small-scale icebergs that make a creepy growling sound when they grind against the hull of a passing ship. These are two of the most common types of ice seen in the Arctic.

This icy tundra is what the **polar bear** calls home.

POLAR BEARS might be one of the largest land mammals alive, but they're also one of the hardest to spot. That's because they're so well camouflaged in the snowy Arctic region, where they live. But I bet you didn't know that polar bears don't really have white fur—every individual hair in a polar bear's coat is actually a clear hollow tube! Each tube traps the sun's energy and channels the heat to the bear's skin, helping to keep him warm in the icy Arctic climate.

Polar bears are carnivores—that means they eat only meat. Their favorite food is the seal, and if you're lucky enough to see a polar bear, you just might find him waiting silently by a seal's breathing hole in the ice, waiting for the seal to come up for air. Polar bears are excellent hunters for a reason; they have a superior sense of sight and smell—they can smell a living meal from as far as twenty miles away. They can be sneaky, too! Polar bears are known to hold up one of their white paws to cover their black noses as they stalk their prey on ice.

These bears are big. They can grow to be up to eleven feet tall and weigh up to 1,600 pounds. But they're definitely not lazy. Polar bears are the most nomadic of all bear species—they travel an average of fifteen miles every day! They can run as fast as twenty-five miles per hour, and they're as comfortable in water as on land. Their water-repellent fur and partially webbed feet make it easy for polar bears to swim and dive to catch underwater prey like sea birds do.

The northern lights
can be as colorful as fireworks!

This colorful display of lights is called the aurora borealis, a natural phenomenon. Auroras occur when energy from the sun interacts with the earth's atmosphere, which is made up of different gases like oxygen and nitrogen.

A picture of the NORTHERN LIGHTS, taken on GUNFLINT LAKE in NORTHERN MINNESOTA.

Here's how it works: the sun is constantly giving off charged particles like protons and electrons, forming the solar wind, which travels away from the sun at speeds of about one million miles per hour. When these speedy particles enter the earth's upper atmosphere, they collide with atoms of atmospheric gases and produce the light that forms *auroras*.

No two auroras are alike—each has a unique shape, size, and color. The color of the light created depends on the type of gas that interacts with the solar wind, and no two gases give off exactly the same colors. The most common aurora is made up of a yellow-green light, and it's a result of the solar wind's collision with oxygen at altitudes of about 100 to 300 kilometers. The color of the aurora can also depend on the height where the solar wind strikes the atmosphere—collisions with those same oxygen atoms at altitudes above 300 kilometers produce rare red auroras.

Why don't you see this display of lights from your backyard? Before the solar wind hits the earth's atmosphere, it's captured by the earth's magnetosphere—the region surrounding our planet formed by the EARTH'S MAGNETIC FIELD. When the charged particles of the solar wind approach the earth, they are drawn to the North or South Pole by the force of this magnetic field before they are able to descend and bump into the atmosphere. That's why the aurora borealis is easily seen at the North Pole, while the South Pole enjoys views of the aurora australis.

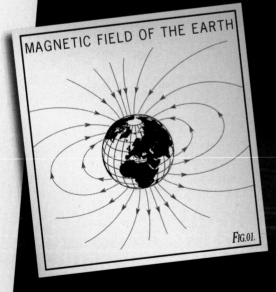

MAGNETIC FIELD OF THE EARTH

FIG.01.

Santa's other airship

Have you ever seen a gigantic blimp fly overhead and wondered how a machine that big could float?

BLIMP.

Blimps and zeppelins are both types of airships that are steerable "lighter-than-air" crafts. What makes a vehicle "lighter-than-air?" That's if the machine uses a lifting gas, like helium, in order to be lighter than the air surrounding it. For the same reason a piece of wood will float in water, the craft floats in the heavier air—that's why the name airship is so perfect! Lifting gas fills out the fabric envelope structure of an air-

ship and makes the machine lift, just like a balloon filled with helium! In fact, an airship is a lot like a giant balloon with an engine, so you can "drive" it through the air instead of having to be carried by the wind.

What's the difference between a blimp and a zeppelin? A zeppelin is called a rigid airship because it has a fixed internal structure that maintains its shape. That structure is covered with a fabric skin. A blimp, however, doesn't have an internal frame. Instead, blimps hold their shape from the pressure of the lifting gas keeping them in the air.

ZEPPELIN.

internal structure

What could be better than a great Christmas present, **all wrapped up?**

KEEP IT SIMPLE WITH STICKERS.
Brighten up plain wrapping paper with whatever stickers you please! Turn red or green paper into a blizzard of polka dots with different colored sticker dots. Or hint at what's inside: teddy bear stickers on a wrapped teddy bear, or train stickers on a toy train set.

Jazz up your gift wrap by using rubber stamp and ink pads. You can make this activity extra fun by creating your own "stamps" out of sponges. Choose cookie cutters in snazzy holiday shapes like stars, Christmas trees, and angels, and then use a thin marker to draw their outlines on some kitchen sponges. Or draw your own shapes. Cut out the outlined shapes with scissors, dip in paint, and stamp away! Not afraid to get a little messy? Use your own fingertips or even hands as stamps!

The **Christmas tree** at the North Pole is one of the most spectacular ever.

THE LEGEND OF THE FIRST CHRISTMAS TREE

In the sixteenth century, a German religious reformer named Martin Luther was walking home late one winter evening near Christmastime. During his stroll, he noticed how beautiful the twinkling stars looked against a background of dark evergreen trees standing tall along his path. He was so awed by the beautiful sight that he decided to recreate the scene for his family. Luther cut down a small evergreen tree and set it up in the main room of his home. He attached candles to the tree's branches, lit them, and declared that this would be a symbol of the Christmas sky.

Jingle bells! Jingle bells!

Do you know what kind of bells those are on Santa's sleigh? They are crotal bells, and they're one of dozens of different types of bells in the world. Bells are one of the oldest musical instruments in history—they've been around for more than 5,000 years. Even before they were used to make music (or announce Santa's arrival), ancient people rang bells and even wore bells during dark winter nights, believing they would scare away evil spirits!

SLEIGH BELLS

Crotal bells are closed hollow spheres with a pellet captured inside—kind of like a walnut. The loose pellet—also called a jinglet or pea—is a small ball usually made of metal that rattles about inside the crotal to sound the bell. All it takes is a little movement to make the bell ring; that's why they jingle with every reindeer movement.

OPEN BELL

CLAPPER

CROTAL BELL

CROTAL

PELLET

The many exciting things the boy saw and learned on his Polar Express journey will live on for years to come in his memory and in this keepsake book of his extraordinary experiences.

POST CARD

PLACE STAMP HERE

POLAR POP

230 ENTRÉ TARIF MUSÉE COLLECTION

Have you ever made a scrapbook of a memorable time in your life? Why not make your next adventure truly unforgettable by creating your own keepsake memory book, so that you can relive the excitement every time you open the cover and flip through its pages?

The pictures you include, the things you write about—they're all up to you. Just remember to keep your eyes, ears, and mind open—after all, you never know when you will find yourself on a journey you'll never want to forget.